Emily's First Day of School

By Sarah, Duchess of York

Illustrated by Ian Cunliffe

STERLING

New York / London

STERLING and the distinctive Sterling logo are registered trademarks of
Sterling Publishing Co., Inc.

Library of Congress Cataloging-in-Publication Data

York, Sarah Mountbatten-Windsor, Duchess of, 1959-
[Holly's first day at school]
Emily's first day of school / by Sarah, Duchess of York ; illustrated by Ian Cunliffe.
p. cm. -- (Helping hand)
Summary: Emily is nervous before her first day of school, but she has such a good time that
she cannot wait until the second day. Includes note to parents.
ISBN 978-1-4027-7392-1
[1. First day of school--Fiction. 2. Schools--Fiction.] I. Cunliffe, Ian, ill. II. Title.
PZ7.Y823Em 2010
[E]--dc22

2009042147

Lot #:
2 4 6 8 10 9 7 5 3 1
04/10
Published by Sterling Publishing Co., Inc.
387 Park Avenue South, New York, NY 10016
Story and illustrations © 2007 by Startworks Ltd
'Ten Helpful Hints' © 2009 by Startworks Ltd
Distributed in Canada by Sterling Publishing
c/o Canadian Manda Group, 165 Dufferin Street
Toronto, Ontario, Canada M6K 3H6
Distributed in Australia by Capricorn Link (Australia) Pty. Ltd.
P.O. Box 704, Windsor, NSW 2756, Australia

Sterling ISBN 978-1-4027-7392-1

For information about custom editions, special sales, premium and
corporate purchases, please contact Sterling Special Sales
Department at 800-805-5489 or specialsales@sterlingpublishing.com.

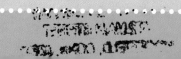

All children face many new experiences as they grow up, and helping them to understand and deal with each is one of the most demanding and rewarding things we do as parents. Helping Hand Books are for both children and parents to read, perhaps together. Each simple story describes a childhood experience and shows some of the ways in which to make it a positive one. I do hope these books encourage children and parents to talk about these sometimes difficult issues. Talking together goes a long way to finding a solution.

Sarah,

Sarah, Duchess of York

Emily's morning should have been like every other one. She would eat breakfast then play with her baby brother Jake while Mommy read the newspaper. But today things were going to be different. From now on, Emily would spend part of every day away from Mommy and Jake.

Today was Emily's first day of school.

A few weeks ago, Emily visited her new school with Mommy and Daddy and Jake. She got to see where the school was and meet Mrs. Anderson, the teacher.

But Emily knew it wouldn't be the same once Mommy and Daddy weren't at school with her. She wouldn't even have Jake to play with.

Emily talked to Amy, her friend Charlotte's big sister, who had been at the school for two years.

"It's great," Amy said. "You'll make lots of friends and Mrs. Anderson is really fun."

Emily thought she might like the idea of meeting some new friends.

Still, on the morning of her first day, everything seemed very strange. Emily felt tears in her eyes as her mommy squeezed her hand in front of the school and said, "You go with Mrs. Anderson now. I will be back this afternoon before you know it."

Emily joined lots of other children who looked just as nervous as she did.

Mrs. Anderson led them along the hallway to the school's gym for an assembly. The gym was big and noisy, full of children talking to one another. Some of them seemed to be older than Emily.

A tall man walked into the room. "Good morning, children. I'm Mr. Wainwright, your school principal," he said. "Welcome back to school. I hope you enjoyed your summer vacation. Let's give a special welcome to the children who are new to our school this year. I know you will all be very happy here."

After the assembly, Mrs. Anderson took the children to their classroom, which Emily remembered from her visit. It was a big room with lots of windows. Emily could see the playground outside.

The classroom had little wooden tables, blue chairs, and a huge pile of building blocks. There were lots of colored things on the walls and a big poster with all the different letters of the alphabet. Emily hoped she'd be able to remember all the letters soon.

On another wall were some children's paintings. Emily loved painting and wondered when she would get to make one of her own. She had lots of ideas—her dog, her house or the tree in front of it, the cow she saw on the farm in the summer, or maybe even the bee that stung her!

Mrs. Anderson gathered everyone in a circle to get to know each other. All the children told the class their names and where they lived.

Emily discovered that her new friend Maria lived just around the corner from her.

They would be able to play together!

The rest of the day passed in a flash: story time, playing, lunch, and art.

"What are you going to draw, Emily?" asked Mrs. Anderson.

Emily looked out the window. "How about the playground?" she asked.

Emily began drawing with her colored pencils. She was so busy that before she knew it, it was time to go home.

Emily was one of the last to come out of the school.
She had been busy putting her pencils away.

"Are you alright, Emily?" asked her mommy. She had
been waiting in front of the school and was becoming a
little nervous.

"Mommy, I'm fine," said Emily.

Then, without stopping, Emily began
to tell her everything about her busy
first day.

Emily couldn't stop talking.

"And then we went to the playground! And Maria came too! We played hopscotch!" she said, hardly taking a breath. "You'll like her, Mommy. Maria's my new best friend!"

"And then we got to draw. I haven't
finished my drawing yet, but I'm going
to do some more tomorrow. Mrs. Anderson says she likes
my picture."

Emily had so many things to say, she was still talking
by the time they got home.

"Well, I'm glad that you had such a busy day, Emily,"
her mommy said. "I told you this morning it was going to
be exciting."

Emily thought about that morning and how she had
felt. It seemed like such a long time ago. Now she couldn't
wait to go to her *second* day of school!

TEN HELPFUL HINTS

FOR PARENTS OF CHILDREN WHO ARE STARTING SCHOOL

By Dr. Richard Woolfson, PhD

1. Don't use school as a threat when your preschooler misbehaves. That gets things off to a bad start, and your child will begin to dislike the thought of school even before she has even started.

2. Let your child ask you questions. In the months leading up to the first day of school, your child will probably ask you what it will be like, about the staff, and about the other children. This is only natural. Try to answer all his questions as best you can.

3. Take your child on a visit to the school at least once before she starts attending regularly. If the school doesn't arrange these visits automatically, make contact with your school directly to set one up.

4. Encourage your child to look around the whole school, not just the classroom. He should view, for instance, the library, the bathrooms, the playground, and the gymnasium. He will be better acquainted with his surroundings if he is able to walk around the entire school.

5. Get your child used to group activities. In the classroom, most learning takes place in group settings, so provide opportunities for her to play with other children her own age at group games and activities. This prepares her for what lies ahead.

6. Sharpen your child's independence skills. Practice the key tasks that he'll need to cope with every day in school, such as taking turns, putting on his coat, completing basic activities without needing assistance, using the bathroom on his own, answering questions, tying his shoes, and eating politely with the other children.

7. Keep her confidence high. Boost your child's self-esteem before starting school by reassuring her that she is a very capable child and that she'll do well at school. Point out her strengths to her. Tell her that the other children will all like her and will want to be her friend.

8. Remain calm on the first day. Your child's first day of school is also a significant event in your own life, and some parents also get upset at this milestone. Try to stay relaxed and happy when taking him there, as he will follow your lead.

9. Always be enthusiastic when talking about school. Your child is heavily influenced by your attitudes and values. If you have a positive and upbeat approach when talking with her about school, the chances are that she will be enthusiastic as well.

10. When you collect your child from school at the end of the first day, ask him lots of questions about what happened there. Give him time to chatter away to you, and respond positively. If he has any concerns at all, give an instant response to show that you are listening and that they can be easily resolved.

Dr. Richard Woolfson is a child psychologist, working with children and their families. He is also an author and has written several books on child development and family life, in addition to numerous articles for magazines and newspapers. Dr. Woolfson runs training workshops for parents and child care professionals and appears regularly on radio and television. He is a Fellow of the British Psychological Society.

Helping Hand Books

Look for these other helpful books to share with your child: